W9-ATS-949

BOFFO

THE GREAT MOTORCYCLE RACE

Frank Dickens

PARENTS' MAGAZINE PRESS / NEW YORK

Frank Dickens, the creator of Boffo, is a well-known English cartoonist and children's book illustrator. *The Great Motorcycle Race* marks Boffo's debut in this country. It is also Dickens's first book for Parents' Magazine Press.

Published by Parents' Magazine Press 1978

10 9 8 7 6 5 4 3 2 1

Library of Congress Cataloging in Publication Data
Dickens, Frank.
Boffo the great motorcycle race.

SUMMARY: Uncle Boffo relates how he won the Great Motorcycle Race with the aid of milk.
[1. Motorcycle racing—Fiction] I. Title.
PZ7.D552Bo1978 [E] 77-22087.
ISBN 0-8193-0956-7 ISBN 0-8193-0957-5 lib.bdg.

BOFFO the Great Motorcycle Race

"Hurry up and drink your milk, children," says Mother.
"Always milk," grumbles William.
"We're sick of it," says Lucy.

Uncle Boffo chuckles from his seat by the window. "Had it not been for milk," he begins, "I would never have won the Great Motorcycle Race...

All the top riders were taking part—Speedy Sam, Legs Eleven, Alan the Hat, and Elephant Bill. But I was riding a cycle of my own design and was sure I could win.

My most dangerous rival was Rudy, a mustachioed villain, who would stop at nothing to win.

B
R

On a long uphill stretch, Rudy and I left the rest far behind.
We were riding neck and neck.

Suddenly Rudy snatched a can of nails from under his sweater and threw it in my path.

Then he rode off, leaving me with two flat tires.
What was I to do—give up?

GIVE UP? NEVER!

Looking around for a solution, I spied a cow in a field — and I knew my problem was solved."

“You rode the cow?” asks William.

“Certainly not,” frowns Uncle Boffo. “That would have been against the rules. I milked it instead,” he says, smiling.

“And you drank the milk to give you energy?” asks Lucy.

Boffo grins and shakes his head.“Wrong again.

MOO!

MOO!

I poured it into the the valves on the flat tires.

Then, pumping up the tires, I sprang into the seat—

B
B

and raced off after Rudy."

“But what about the flat tires?” ask the children.
“Repaired.”
“Repaired how?” they insist.

"By the milk," chuckles Boffo. "What happens when you spin milk?"

"It turns to butter," cries Lucy.

"Exactly. And when the wheels of my motorcycle spun round, the milk turned to butter and sealed up all the holes.

Knowing that my tires were repaired, I was able to catch Rudy just before the finish. He was none too pleased, I can tell you."

"But how could you catch him when he was so far ahead?" asks William.

“Easily,” says Boffo. “He had been held up by a herd of cows.”

And Uncle Boffo begins to laugh until tears roll down his cheeks.
"Would you children like something else to drink?" asks Mother.

"Yes, Mother," cry Lucy and William.
"MORE MILK, PLEASE."